Usborne
Phonics Readers
Goose on the loose

Phil Roxbee Cox

Illustrated by Stephen Cartwright

Edited by Jenny Tyler

Language consultant: Marlynne Grant

BSc, CertEd, MEdPstch, PhD, AFBPs, CPsychol

There is a little yellow duck to find on every page.

First published in 2006 by Usborne Publishing Ltd., Usborne House, 83-85 Saffron Hill, London EC1N 8RT, England. www.usborne.com
Copyright © 2006, 2001 Usborne Publishing Ltd.

Goose is on a scooter.
She can't stay and play.

She's a goose on the loose.
"Get out of my way!"

HONK!

She almost runs down Rooster Ron.

"Get out of my way!"
Goose goes scooting on.

HONK!
HONK!

Goose is scooting to Ted's shed...

Ted ends up in his flower bed.

...own the road.

She almost scoots
right into Toad.

The cows all moo.

The doves all coo.

10

HONK HONK!

Look out! Goose is on the loose.

She upsets a bunch of kangaroos...

...and shocks a flock of cockatoos.

There are shouts of "hiss!"
and shouts of "boo!"

Then snarls and howls
and a hullabaloo.

"Goose must be stopped! What shall we do?"

But Goose has stopped, and feels a fool.

She's landed in the penguin pool!